I0451790

CABBAGE
LANGUAGE

robert duncan gray

HOUSEFIRE

www.housefirebooks.com

ISBN: 978-1-937395-03-2

Copyright 2013 HOUSEFIRE

Cover art copyright 2013 Robert Duncan Gray

Interior layout by Riley Michael Parker

THE SON OF THE SUN edited by Riley Michael Parker and Lindsay Allison Ruoff

AMATEUR PORNOGRAPHY edited by Robyn Bateman and Lindsay Allison Ruoff

All rights reserved. No part of this book may be reproduced or transmitted in any form or by any means, electronic or mechanic, without the written consent of the publisher, except for excerpts for the purpose of review or where permitted by law.

Portions of this book have previously appeared in the following publications: STOKED, UP Literature and Small Doggies Magazine. Sincere thanks to these fine publishers for their support.

Printed in 'merica.

P R A I S E

for CABBAGE LANGUAGE and Robert Duncan Gray

CABBAGE LANGUAGE will turn you over. It will put you where you need to be. It will teach you all of the new positions—even the ones you're afraid to know.

Scott McClanahan, author of
THE COLLECTED WORKS OF
SCOTT MCCLANANHAN VOL. 1
(Lazy Fascist Press)

In reading CABBAGE LANGUAGE, I felt as though I was ready to celebrate the end of the world with Solomon Thunderbeast, a new bleak hero in the literary canon. CABBAGE LANGUAGE continues to floor me in its perfect phrases, each one spare, beautiful, and often so very funny. Sentence by sentence, I never wanted it to stop.

Richard Chiem, author of
YOU PRIVATE PERSON
(Scrambler Books)

P R A I S E

for CABBAGE LANGUAGE and Robert Duncan Gray

Alphabets of madness, cabinets of curiosities and absurdity contortions, Robert Duncan Gray spins startling detail and surreal juxtaposition into something alchemical and right for our beautiful times. There is revolution here, he warns us, nestled neatly in the shadows. We should heed his words.

M. Bartley Seigel, author of
THIS IS WHAT THEY SAY
(Typecast Publishing)
and founding editor of [PANK]

———————————

AMATEUR PORNOGRAPHY is a collection of poems about death, everyday life, and the absence of friends. It is the perfect antidote to those who do not have an OkCupid account.

Janey Smith, author of
ANIMALS
(Plain Wrap Press)

THE SON OF THE SUN

-page five-

amateur pornography

-page one hundred and seventeen-

THE SON OF THE SUN

a novella in five parts

part one

the world inside

I

Before everything, sperm.

Like honey. A swarm of marine life.

How we move.

The scenery. . . marvelous!

Marathon rain dance toward the light. How it begins just
as it ends.

The victory of one fish.

Time. Time. Growth. Time.

The squeeze.

Sudden cold. So cold. I cry and I cry and I cry.

Some childhood.

Strange growth. Hair.

Erection. Friction. Ejaculation.

This is the best.

This is the worst.

The best and the worst at the same time, all the time.

II

Memory fails me. It was an accident. This is what is happening.

Pure white walls. A window with open orange curtains in front of a chair made of beige plastic. I sit with a straight spine, staring out, perfectly lit from all angles—the daylight coming in through the window and the warm light of old electricity on my back. I sit and I focus.

Outside there is a garden. Roses and potatoes. I am not looking at anything. I am looking at nothing.

For the sake of spoiling dessert, let it be known that this ends in the rain. This ends in a tangle of concrete and metal. Last night it became clear that if I do not write this, nobody will. And if it is not written, it will not be remembered. I suppose that wouldn't be so bad, but it would be a waste. A waste of life. We are people and this is a place and we deserve to be written about as much as anything else, so I am going to write. I'm the best speller here, anyway.

III

I am frowning now, remembering a time I was smiling.
I hardly recognize my self. This is simple truth. There is
a window and I am looking through it and I see what I
believe to be a reflection, but not mine. Another person is
looking back at me. I am not sure of this other person.

His hair is a mess.

IV

I turn away from the window and the world outside. The
oak trees have been swing dancing birds into the wind
but stopped not half a minute ago, so I allow my gaze
to settle on Wimbledon's face as he shouts at The Lady
with Long Legs about his breakfast. I LIKE MY TOAST
BURNT. I TOLD YOU THIS MORNING. WHAT DO
YOU NOT UNDERSTAND? BURNT. BURNT LIKE
FUCKING CREMATED and she's all shook up but he's
almost laughing, really. She hasn't learned his faces yet.
Sometimes Wimbledon's face looks like the opposite of
what it really is. I don't feel much in the way of sorry
for her. I heard him say the word CREMATED quite
clearly this morning. Wimbledon likes most of his food
blackened, his bacon so burnt it crumbles to a touch.
Perhaps she didn't get much sleep last night.

The light is always perfect. Everywhere you look there's a
photograph.

One would never guess at first glance, but there is freedom
here. It doesn't look like it, but we live as if we were
guests at a mediocre hotel. We have cable television,
though it has lost its appeal since last year's spectacle.
The commercials are lazy. Too much discussion of who

is and who is not a real person, and who might be an animal or something worse. But really, everything here is perfect. We have each other. We have sex, or at least some equivalent of sex. I am provided my drug of choice. I am encouraged to change my mind. My thoughts belong to me. We have ping pong and music, books to read and something real to rebel against: The General. We are united in the fact that we live because The General lets it be so. He keeps us here. Perhaps he is a necessity just as much as the windows. Whether or not his presence and power is oppressive—that is to say, against our will—is up for debate. Some days are like cheap wine; they stain the teeth. He provides for us, simultaneously playing god and the devil, always holding hands with himself behind his back. His mustache is typically impressive. His vocabulary, cabbage. The mozzarella is sweating, he says.

We play ping pong almost every day. Mostly I am the best, though I have been off my game lately. Wimbledon is crap. Robert Lee is almost tied with me, but I'm the champion. The brothers hardly play anymore, but when they do they're both mid range. When The General was here last week I played against him. I whittled him in the first game and lost on purpose in the second, but everyone who was watching knows I lost on purpose. We all know what's what around here, even when we don't say so out loud. He was already embarrassed enough. He probably would have had me shot if I had beaten him twice in a row. I saved his face for everyone's sake, mostly my own. That being said, sometimes I don't think I'd mind being shot as much as I should. Sometimes the toast is not bread at all.

This place has strange politics. The system is balanced haphazardly. Imagine a library built by a blind student of carpentry. In our free time we plan wild escapes, but that's mostly just horse shit. There's no point, really. We're better off in here than we are out there.

I'd rather be looking out a window than into one.

V

I suppose I should offer a better description of what's going on here.

I'll try to justify ourselves for you.

We are sort of a gang. I like thinking about it like that. We were drawn here by various forces outside our control and we have ended up here together and that makes us sort of a gang.

My name is Thunderbeast, Solomon Thunderbeast, which is the name I chose for myself. I got both parts of my name from different television shows. I do not know what my real name is.

I am a beard growing type of man. Inside my beard I keep diamonds and a weapon, a family I can't remember, and my sadness. I do not recognize my sadness, I just feel it like an itch on my back that I cannot comfortably reach. I often wish I was someone else, someone with handfuls of young flesh and a soft voice and infinite money—someone on television. I occasionally develop a longing for a third nipple or some odd birthmark. I snap out of it and realize I am fully erect again and the coffee has gone cold. There was an accident. It was my fault. Something of love and death. I do not understand the language of happiness and sadness. That's how best I can explain myself from my own perspective.

Robert Lee is here too, so if there is a gang, he's in it. He is named after his father who is named after Robert E. Lee, a general—not The General, another one. Robert Lee's best friend in middle school was a girl called Ethel Greenglass. She was the first girl he ever fingered, years before she was put to death for falling in love with an unlucky communist. It was around the time she died that Robert decided Ethel was his number one girl and he was all broken up about it. He was diagnosed some time early on, but when the government couldn't sustain his budget he went from being schizo to just plain old homeless crazy. Now he's here with us. I like Robert Lee.

Wimbledon came from some small place in the middle of America that had the Red Scare real bad so everyone in the neighborhood had a fallout shelter. Wimbledon's fallout shelter was stocked with a week's worth of food and water and all the other fallout shelter fixings, including a loaded gun and a radio that didn't have any batteries. One day there was a false alarm and the whole family fled into their bunker. His old man was a little loose in the head about the bomb. Since the radio had no batteries, they didn't get the message that it was a false alarm and the old man wouldn't let them out. Days dragged on and the food went and they all started to get a little crazed with malnourishment and cabin fever and wild thoughts about what might have happened to old America above their heads. What happened happened. Wimbledon doesn't speak about it. I learned all this from

The Lady with Long Legs. She told me he was the only one that left the fallout shelter on his own two feet. The rest were lying down. I don't ask questions. Whatever happened in that bunker is between Wimbledon and his dead family.

I truthfully don't know shit about the brothers, except that even though they don't talk, each always knows what the other is thinking. They're a couple Russians, I think. Maybe Polish. At least they look Eastern European and I think they have one of those funny sounding names, something like a bad guy in a film, which escapes me at this moment.

VI

The light of day is a sort of pen pal of mine. I write her letters, the old way.

Dear Light,

I watch you shine through windows. I watch the shadows you create swim across the room. I feel your heat and I miss you when you're gone. Why won't you speak to me? I have read your letter a thousand times over, the paper is starting to melt every time I unfold it. Your silence is torture, more so than anything else that is happening here.

My days, though numbered, are monotonous. I write this letter from my deathbed, though I am not sick and I am not dying. This is my bed and I am waiting for death, that's all. The afternoon guard told me The General signed the forms last week, but nothing has happened yet. Sometimes the paperwork is not even necessary—these things slip through the cracks. Good men get lost even when no forms have been signed. It can happen with a snap from his fingers, so I don't understand the hold up. I want to get it over and done with. Being in this place without more of you. Hell is to wait.

Send good news. Send love.

Sincerely yours,

Solomon Thunderbeast

Any kind of love is warm. Even imaginary love can keep a man alive.

VII

Robert Lee gets real scared when the telephone rings. He can't shake the feeling that it's going to kill him. When he really flips the switch, he shouts TRYING TO KILL ME WITH A TELEPHONE, FUCK FUCK FUCK over and over, which usually happens at night and it's as real as anything else. People think he's fallen off his horse, but he told me the story, and having heard his side, I conclude that Robert Lee is in his right mind more than anyone I know. I would live scared too if I shared his sickness, which is not really a sickness at all, just what his life is.

Robert Lee was a celebrating sort of man in his previous incarnation. He drank what he could find and often found himself in places most people actively avoid. One day, when he was in one of those places, he got caught with his hand on the wrong woman's tit. He was trying to claim a tit that in actual fact belonged to a woman who belonged to some Mexican mafia boss, so Robert Lee got beat. After getting beat he got threatened left and right, including over the telephone. So he's scared the telephone'll kill him, because the telephone told him so. Over and over and over.

VIII

Wimbledon speaks cool. Sometimes it's as if an action film is playing in his head and he blurts out the slickest lines at random. The words he chooses often have no anchor in the real world. Like he'll be eating fried eggs, all burnt the way he likes it, and suddenly he'll shout NEVER LET THE HARVEST MOON RISE OVER YOUR ABYSS, PILGRIM, or THERE'S A FUCKING GRENADE IN MY ASS AND I'M GETTING TIRED OF CLENCHING!

We have learned to ignore it, for the most part.

IX

Everything feels fragile

like if I miss breakfast
it might cause an earthquake,

or if I forget to say I LOVE YOU
I might forget how.

Whatever controls the weather conspires with whatever
controls the planets
and their new goal is to crush the human spirit.

But everywhere, even here,
everywhere is music.

X

The Lady with Long Legs has a name. I don't remember
it, so I call her The Lady with Long Legs. I could probably
remember it if I wanted. That is to say, I choose not to
remember it. It's not because of the accident.

The General comes into our living quarters once every
few weeks stone drunk. He cups The Lady with Long
Legs's buttocks with both hands and she can't stop him
because he's The General. Plus she knows he's just being
a bastard. He would never fuck her. He is too afraid of
his wife. I guess he's just being an asshole. It's best to
avoid eye contact with him when he's drunk like that. He's
looking for someone to start something. An excuse to call
in the firing squad.

I smoked a joint with the morning guard last week. We
talked shit on The General, but later I heard that the
morning guard got caught stealing ice cream from the
officer's fridge and got his good hand cut off.

The temptation to bite the hand that feeds you strengthens
thanks to the inedibility of the food it serves.

XI

I feel colonial. There has been an obtuse angle inside
my chest since last night. I took a second shower having
forgotten my first. The angle at which I saw my hands
holding the soap gave me a flashback and I realized I was
already clean. Too clean. Raw pink skin. I asked Robert
Lee how many times I took a shower. He said SEVEN.
MAYBE EIGHT.

Every time somebody dies, it gives me a headache. I
remember them by remembering the food they ate and
what stains never washed out of their clothing. The smell
of strangers' sweat enflames memories of people whose
faces I cannot place. These people stare at me.

XII

My darling,

I woke up yesterday afternoon in the kitchen. I couldn't remember falling asleep. I had a dream about the night we spent together. Your cheeks like grapefruits. I held you in my arms and felt like a man for the first time in my life.

I live in fear that you are dead, because I can think of no other reason for your silence. I believe you would write if you could. You told me you would with the same look in your eyes as when you told me you loved me. If one was a lie, both were a lie. And you have not written. If I choose to believe you, I must believe you are dead. But the truth is I love you and I hope you are alive and hope you lied to me because I don't want you to be dead. You, my love, deserve to live forever.

Always,
Solomon

XIII

If there are drugs in the house, I will do them. They will be done by me.

Today I have exhaled over 13 thousand times. I counted.

I ate my first apricot. It was OK.

I asked for a vanilla milkshake and was given grief.

I don't want to come off as an asshole. Though upon reflection, I am a bit of an asshole.

This morning it seems to be both sunny and rainy. Fox wedding weather. The cat is not hungry, so perhaps he knows what's going on. It is a Wednesday. The liars are outside. The abyss is a mere bike ride away, but here I am, on the edge. Safe, plush, flaccid.

I cried all over the building and spilled out onto the streets. I told the men I had been drinking, which was true. I don't know why I'm here or what we're doing. I only know that we are not going anywhere. We are stuck! Stuck! Stuck! Stuck!

part two
the madness of the general

I will dedicate the alphabet to
the madness of The General.

It's time you get to know him better.

A

I saw a dog with three legs crossing Main at Sixth. The forth paw hung loose as if recently broken, held an inch from the ground, dangling grotesquely. I usually like three legged animals, but found the dangling appendage repulsive. What's often best is a good clean break. Who needs loose skin?

B

IF YOU SEE SOMETHING, SAY SOMETHING, the
voice of The General crackles through invisible speakers.
He has been listening to *Stasiland* on tape and has all
kinds of fun new paranoias floating around his head. He's
trying to turn us into communists, just so that he can
torture false confessions out of us. He loves a good reason
to torture. His false idols are obvious. They are yesterday's
dictators. The villains of history. He's harmless though, if
you play him right. So he wants us to be commies. Maybe
we'll be commies. Why not, you know? It's not like we
need to be anything else.

C

He came rushing into the house shouting MY PENIS MY
PENIS MY PENIS HAS FALLEN OFF! He was wearing
his red pajamas, and, contrary to his claims, his penis
was not only attached but actually exposed, hanging out
of an opening, a gap in the sea of red cotton where two
consecutive buttons had fallen off, the thing flapping
around like that three-legged dog's useless paw. MY
PENIS HAS FALLEN OFF! He rushed into the bathroom,
our bathroom that is, and lay in the bathtub, curled into the
fetal position, and fell asleep. In the morning, he slept in
later than any of us. He was sucking his thumb.

D

The General once purchased some sort of tribal pygmy man from the heart of one of those jungles you read about, but got sick of him after a few days and returned him on account of being "too big."

E

There are spiderwebs everywhere. Fucking everywhere. Spiderwebs, but no spiders. Not one.

F

This morning I woke up to find the General sitting at the foot of my bed, staring at me, smiling. I said GOOD MORNING and he told me he had something to tell me. I HAVE SOMETHING TO TELL YOU, he said. I remained silent, hoping perhaps that my paperwork had gone through and this whole thing would be over soon. This was not the case. He told me he was my father. I asked him his age. He said fifty-three. I told him that if this was true he would have been six years old when he had me, probably five at the time of conception. He told me he was. WHAT ABOUT OUR STRIKINGLY DIFFERENT ETHNICITIES, I asked. He slapped me in the face, told me he loved me unconditionally, and left.

G

The General has been known to disappear for weeks
at a time without telling anyone where he is going.
Some say he goes overseas, some say he just doesn't
leave his bedroom. He is crazy enough to be anywhere.
ANYWHERE.

H

There are hidden cameras here, all around us. They are hidden in plain view. There is a birdhouse in the living room with a protruding camera lens placed awkwardly in the middle of a wooden pane. None of them appear to be plugged into any power source. They are just there, offering paranoia.

I

One time, the General's penis actually did fall off. The Lady with Long Legs told me. He had it surgically enhanced, but something went wrong and the tip came off in his hand when he was taking a piss. She swore on her mother's grave.

J

The late afternoon guard suffered a terrible fate. The General came in on his watch and addressed him in a formal manner. Salute. Salute. AT EASE.

YOU ARE THE MAN WITH THE SPLENDID FAMILY, AREN'T YOU, SOLDIER?

YES, GENERAL.

WELL, SOLDIER. I HAVE TAKEN A FANCY TO YOUR WIFE. SHE WILL BE MINE NOW.

GENERAL?

YOUR WIFE, SOLDIER. SHE IS NOW MY WIFE.

BUT YOU HAVE A WIFE.

NOT ANY MORE. MY WIFE IS DEAD. I NEED A NEW ONE AND I WANT YOURS.

The room stretched like a rubber band. Robert Lee, Wimbledon, the guard, and I stared at The General's condescending smirk smeared across his cheeks. He broke the silence with a loud fart and waved his hand behind his ass, fanning the smell toward me.

BRING HER TO ME. NOW.

YES, GENERAL. PLEASE, GENERAL, WHAT ABOUT MY FAMILY? OUR CHILDREN?

I DO NOT WANT YOUR DISGUSTING CHILDREN, SOLDIER. I ONLY WANT YOUR WIFE.

YES, GENERAL.

The afternoon guard left the room, presumably in the direction of his quarters. Several minutes later, we heard gunshots. It was the guard trying to escape, trying to smuggle his wife out. He was shot dead and she was escorted to The General, who was waiting, patiently examining my bonsai tree.

KNEW HE'D TRY TO ESCAPE. THE COWARD.

The General glanced at his new wife, an unattractive plump woman in her early forties.

NO, NO. NOT THIS ONE. WHY WOULD I WANT THIS ONE? I WANT THE OTHER ONE. THE ONE WITH THE BOSOM! THE HUGE BOSOM! BRING ME THAT ONE!

The early evening guard began to shrink into the corner.

K

Last week he decided to start smoking. Pall Malls. He
smoked three-quarters of one cigarette before giving up.
He threw the pack in the recycling. I fished it back out.
Now I sit, smoking failure after failure, watching clouds
surrounded by clouds.

L

Laughter. Laughterer. Laughterest. These are three of the General's words. Another word he has is irrespectable. Another is lightning, which means a box of matches or perhaps a candle, depending on the context.

So, his vocabulary is cabbage, yes, but he is not entirely stupid. He knows the value of life. The General knows that when it's his time to die, it will be at the hands of his own people. He must. He expects to meet and greet death like an old friend.

M

The General's children are in crisis placement. He has no concept of them as people. They are an idea that bores him. We were talking drunk about fatherhood when he admitted that he could not recall the conception of any of his children. He couldn't remember the fucking at all. It didn't seem important. He said he secretly avoided sex and dreaded his wife's body. It had always repulsed him, even when they were young. He kept calling her vagina THAT THING and her breasts THOSE THINGS. He said he knew that they had sex, he just couldn't recall it. He couldn't create a visual memory of their bodies together, having been thinking about something else at the time. I told him I knew what he meant and we nodded together.

I guess I knew what he meant.

N

I woke to the sound of a man crying outside the open window that hangs over my bed. My dreamcatcher was rattling in the morning breeze. As I lifted myself up to see who it was, I pulled a muscle in my groin. It was him, The General. He saw me before I could retreat; said nothing. I saw his tears. I saw him being human. I believe I may have damaged his libido and I believe this may be the end for me. The paperwork won't take long now. I am nervous.

O

The death of an animal carries more weight than that of a man around here. A buck was found dead, poisoned by the sewage running into the lake. Robert Lee found it and told me. We dragged it to safety, some place in the trees where the General wouldn't find it easily. We sawed off the antlers. My hands were sweaty. It was more difficult than I imagined.

When we were done we covered the body in leaves and left it to rot, funeral ceremony pending. I hid the antlers in the loose floorboard beneath my bed. True bone is worth more than gold to the right man. We will have to pay a visit to the shaman, the young one. He has a thing for antlers and who can blame him? A beautiful bone. A bone he will pay good money for. I like good money, but I am not looking forward to the exchange. The young shaman is an idiot and, at best, a liability. I will not speak of him. The General must know nothing.

P

The General has caught wind that I have been writing. He talked to me last night. First I thought he was going to confiscate this document, but it turns out he wants me to be his ghostwriter.

I WISH TO COMPOSE AN AUTOBIOGRAPHY. I NEED YOUR HELP. YOU WILL WRITE ME.

I asked if he had made any progress yet.

ONLY A TITLE: MY FIGHT.

I asked if he didn't think that a little too close to the title of Adolf Hitler's book.

WHO?

ADOLF HITLER, SIR.

WHO?

HITLER, SIR GENERAL. ADOLF HITLER.

WHO?

Q

My telephone sure has been acting strange these past few days. It has been listening to me. I can hear it breathing. I hold it to my ear like a seashell. Robert Lee is getting kind of weird, too. He grips a dirty nickel between two cigarette-scarred fingertips, slips it into the front left pocket of his oil-stained jeans and, with a toothless smile, explains that he is saving all his money so that when he dies and goes to heaven he can give it to his mother. He has been smoking the cat's hair.

Robert Lee is the person with whom I have spent the most time discussing death. I once tempted him from the edge of the abyss with a cold cheeseburger. Sometimes he tries to end his life just to fuck with me.

Robert Lee won a coloring book with an accompanying set of crayons in a bingo game and told me
he is saving his prize for his unborn children whom he expects to father after marrying the love of his life. He expects to meet her any day now.

He will never meet this person. He will lose the coloring book or he will give it to me or I will take it.

R

The General goes kayaking on weekends at the local indoor swimming pool. I have never seen it. The pool is elsewhere—outside my world. I only know what The Lady with Long Legs tells me. He rents out the entire establishment and paddles around for an hour or two, smoking cigars and ashing into the chlorinated water. Locals complain amongst themselves during the hot months, but nobody speaks up. Arguing with him is like shaking hands with an exotic bird. This is all hearsay, of course. People talk. I don't know what's true and truth be told I don't care much either.

S

THE GENERAL IS A SWEET, SWEET MAN, say the old women who go to the church in the concrete brick building at the bottom of the hill. How the poor man lost his beautiful wife, how we should feel sorry for him, all alone in his giant mansion. They say he plays the banjo. They say he is a watercolor painter. They think he cooks for himself.

Those of us who are not blind know other truths. We know the trees lean away from the outer walls of his home. The birds never land on his gutters. Lizards do not dare creep his walls. Dogs cease to bark outside the black gates of his driveway. Everyone hurries past the mansion, voices hushed, sometimes not daring to breathe until around the corner.

T

The General is slowly turning into wood, worrying about the shape of things to come and taking deep gulps of various beverages. He drinks White Russians, but calls them something different. With lunch, he prefers bourbon. The later it gets, the more it doesn't matter. He drinks everything.

U

The Lady with Long Legs is in charge of laundry. She does everyone's, including The General's. Here is a list of the items she has found in the pockets of his corduroys:

A plastic walkie-talkie toy designed for ages 3+
A piece of toilet paper with a drawing of a penis in fluorescent yellow
A bundle of dollar bills, totaling $2200, which she successfully kept with no repercussions
An old Nazi medal of honor
A severed human finger
A broken bottle opener
A pacifier
A half empty pack of penis enlargement pills
A ZZ TOP concert stub
A shrimp taco
The spirit of a coyote

I know, I know. I asked her what that was. WHAT DO YOU MEAN BY THE SPIRIT OF A COYOTE, but she wouldn't elaborate. She just started crying. The mind boggles.

V

The General's favorite album is Horses. His second favorite is Blue. His third is Seasons in the Abyss.

W

I like The General. Don't let anything I have written here give you the impression that I do not like him. I liken him to the flesh of an avocado.

X

I am sick. My mind's not right. I am concerned for my mental health. I believe I have cancer—some sort of cancer or perhaps something worse. My mind is stuck in a downward spiral. Professionals probably call this a cycle.

The worst of us. The very worst, most despicable. The child rapists, the gratuitous murderers. They are a part of us. A part of each and every one of us. Buried deep inside the subconscious. Your mother, your father, your sisters and brothers. They are filled with the same scum as I am. The same scum as The General, Adolf Hitler, the postman, the lonely nun writing letters, Robert E. Lee, Samuel Beckett, Margaret Thatcher, the bus driver, Wimbledon, the shoplifter, the village pervert, Frank Hinton, the snowman, the three-legged dog, Jo-Jo the dog-faced boy, his owner, Stanley Kubrick, Vladimir Putin, the knife that twists, the bullet, the bomb, everything just doing its job.

It's enough to make you sick.

Y

When the fruit is ripe, the whole neighborhood sings
something awful good. It's not my business—I shouldn't
have mentioned it—but it is sort of beautiful.

Z

The severity of the capsize
depends on the size and design
of the vessel.

From this perspective
the difference between a man
and a yacht

is being taught to pray
to whatever is invisible,
whatever can fit between clenched teeth,

sweaty palms,
the pages of a book,
or nothing at all.

part three

information overload until pattern recognition

PREFACE

Two items of interest have recently come to light: a photograph and a notebook filled with poetry, apparently written by my hand before the accident. This is the worst news I have received since forgetting everything. I fancied myself a poet. Nothing good will come of this.

In the interest of satisfying curiosity, I will reproduce the poetry for you, in its entirety, forthwith.

January 2

The tambourine player who lives next door has been
practicing all day.
There are diamonds in the rhythm. Echoes of shit.
Shit echoes.
I finish a glass of milk and consider buying a trumpet.
The landlady taps her foot, shakes her keys,
smacks her lips.
Some baby is crying, not ours. We don't have a baby
but I could sleep to this.

January 8

Even though it is not the truth,
I would like to be remembered as
a cigarette smoker.

I'll pick up a discarded butt
and hold it as if it were the part of me I love the most
and you take a photograph.

Make it look nonchalant.
It'll be the sixth finger on my left hand,
an extension of my personality,
as I place it to my lips and hope not to catch something.

Make sure I'm in frame and focus. Make it good.
We're only doing this once.

January 20

Some babies resemble ginger root.
I'm more asphalt.
I grow up and antlers sprout
everywhichway.

January 27

Some beautiful things:

Vegetarian brothel
Open for business
Ancient profession

The bone structure of
A conversation between
A dead cat and a bag of dogs

March 14

A beautiful pervert invites you to share a peach
as if the sun has fallen.

He says WHAT CAN I SAY and you begin to offer
suggestions:

You say
SLAP SOMETHING SILLY AND CALL ME SUSAN or
ONE SIXTEEN OUNCE LATTE WITH SKIMMED
MILK, PLEASE or
I MISS YOU VERY MUCH or
MY THIGHS, LIKE TIGERS, ACHE or
I BOUGHT YOU A BOOK BUT DECIDED TO KEEP IT
FOR MYSELF.

SHUT UP he says

He picks at the fruit with dirty fingers.

March 14

I wear swan feathers like a baseball cap

High five myself

Drink Mountain Dew

High five myself again

I have not been sleeping well

Ideas keep me awake
like cartoons, polyester
icicles, driftwood
pantomime, synthetic family listens to
techno music, talking panthers
black panthers, other panthers

I can't shake right

March 14

From the perspective of a mosquito
through the window of a moving train
halfway between home and the last thing you ate
greens blur
your face looks quite like a smiling face
cheeks flushed with orgasm
Olde English laugh
landlocked
and lager stained
you smell like yesterday's cigarettes and somebody else
who
in retrospect
I do not like

March 14

Listened to the radio one too many minutes
now my baby does the hankypanky
and won't shut up about it.

This black kid dressed royal blue
bounces a basketball and smiles big.
Teeth like pearls
not at all like my teeth.

I KNOW WHAT YOU DID IN THERE.
I SAW THROUGH THE WINDOW.

Glad you enjoyed the show.

The temperature is moderate
but it just started raining.

The sky is the same color as dry oil on driftwood.

The church is sinking.

The shape of genitals.

The rules we broke

twice, three times.

March 15

A girl with plastic ovaries is riding the bus
wearing a tattooed wedding ring and sunshine
on the small of her back.

She speaks Spanish into the palm of her left hand.
Her hair curls shoulder length like snakes.

I catch her eye.
It feels like we are fucking.
I look away prematurely.

She gets off.

I watch through the dirty bus window,
whispering apologies as she walks away.

March 18

Silence
like a bible
forgotten on a train,
a bicycle ride through the rain.

March 21

The subtle art of sinking teeth into concrete.

Teach me how to miss the past.
How to drink chocolate milk.

A horse with antlers ain't a horse
unless they're made of silk.

April 1

My favorite color is tarantula dancing tarantella.
I carry an empty bag just in case.
I carry lungs
kidneys
wishbones
boners
nipples
rings on fingers
fingernails
the eye
stock options
causalities
pitch perfect
forgetfulness
and below everything,
regret

and I ride a bicycle.

May 1

It happens naturally

like cheating in cards against a blind man,

like the opposite of shaving.

The restlessness of the weekendend
and the weight of the weekbeginning.

like sometimes
you can already feel Monday morning
on Friday afternoon,

like patiently waiting
for your lover to fall in love
with somebody else.

If you expect an apology,
you probably don't deserve one.

Can you lend some lightning please for smoking?

POSTSCRIPT

This concludes the poetry. The rest of the pages are blank, except a series of six numbers penciled haphazardly on the back of the last page: 828489. I have read the entire manuscript twice. This is what I have gleaned:

Poetry is dumb. It amazes me that there is even a word for it. Such waste, such a bamboozling of human spirit. The hierarchy of smite in the face of suffering. Poetry is a snake in the sock drawer. Even this right here, these words—me writing them here where I am (in space and time) and you reading them here where you are—is inadequate communication. We don't get it. The translation from writing to reading is bound to miss. The words go through too much travel. You are reading a mistranslation of my moment. The results are wrong so the entire process is counterproductive. We are both doing dumb things, you and I.

So when I read these poems, apparently written by my hand, I miss myself. Who is this? Who is that?

Furthermore, who is allowed to do this and why? Who gave me permission and authority to write? This is not an oracle bone, but it may as well be. Some tiny Stone Henge or some tombstone chiseling. What is this? What is its function?

Bad answer: everything for god and the goodness that is and always has been invisible.

Good answer: nothing and none for no reason.

No. This is bullshit and talk. Thanks to the book, I have only learned backwards. The photograph, however, has taught me this:

My lover had brown hair.

And my parents or perhaps her parents were very short in stature that they may have been Little People, though I can't be positive exactly who and how tall they were—just a series of wild guesses, really.

And my name. The photograph has taught me my name.

part four

everything
is porcelain

1

Some things have changed.

The General is being led out to the courtyard. The drums are rolling in a lighthearted sort of way. Just drums, no other instruments, no voices, no words. The drums are singing THE KING IS DEAD. It is a rhythm that begins to dictate one's pulse and allows the body to hover just above ground level. THE KING IS DEAD.

Nobody is saying LONG LIVE THE KING. Nobody feels shame. This man is a motherfucker. This motherfucker deserves to die.

2

Robert Lee just learned a valuable lesson in linguistics.
Throughout his entire life up until this morning,
he believed that in order for a man to be called A
MOTHERFUCKER, that man had to have fucked
his mother. It wasn't until I called The General a
motherfucker in polite conversation that he recognized the
fiction of the word.

WHAT? THE GENERAL? FUCKED HIS MOTHER?

NO. HE DIDN'T FUCK HIS MOTHER. HE'S JUST A
MOTHERFUCKER.

And then we had a long talk.

Turns out, Robert Lee did actually fuck his mother. One
time only. It was not his proudest moment, but it was
a moment, and though he is not a motherfucker, he is,
in fact, a mother fucker. A one-time fucker of mother.
He has always been sensitive to this fact. He has been
called motherfucker his entire life — mostly by perfect
strangers — always assuming they knew his secret. The
shame must have been such an unbelievable burden. He
never realized that he just lived amongst a whole bunch

of motherfuckers who just fucking hung out calling each other motherfucker for the hell of it. He always felt a sting.

Since learning that motherfucker is a perfectly acceptable word to use and in no real way is directly connected to the fucking of one's mother, or not really anyway, Robert Lee has said it out loud over four hundred times. We only talked a couple of hours ago.

The motherfucker's over the moon.

3

There is revolution here. It is nestled neatly within the scope of The General's shadow.

4

The rose garden needs a trim. One can direct the growth of a rose bush by trimming with the future in mind. Cut away the paths you don't want to follow. Allow the chosen vine to grow and lean toward the sun. Keep a light touch, use the ghosts of your fingernails. Never touch the flower. These are not really rules. Well, maybe they are. I don't know. This is just how I like to think about it, as if it were something sacred, a ritual. The flowers are worthless and so they are precious—more than petal and stem. There is a magic about them.

My potatoes are sprouting. I can grow a hundred pounds of potato in four square feet. Perhaps that's one of the real reasons I am kept alive. My bounty is fat.

5

Light of Day,

I remain restless, even when you wrap your arms around me. You are here but you are nowhere, so I remain restless. My legs kick in spasms. My muscles twitch outside my control. I listened to the wind yesterday for hours. I was high. It helped.

Where are you now? When you are not here, who do you wrap your arms around? I am haunted.

When you are gone, I am afraid you will never come back. You will realize that the other side of the world is where you belong and you will never shine here again. We do not deserve you, that's the truth. The sooner you realize that, the sooner this charade will come to an end.

For you. Always for you,

Solomon

6

I have been unusually tired as of late and dreaming strange. Last night, I dreamt of the perfect vagina. Perfect. Soft. Flower petals. It was wet before I touched it. Wet at the idea of me. When I put my penis to its opening, it gasped for joy. I allowed the weight of my body to press my penis inside. I slid in easily. It should have been perfect, aesthetically it was, but I felt nothing. No sensation. I woke in a cold sweat. I am scared. I am scared.

7

Robert Lee is dying.

He is not sick. He shows no signs of death, but he is
dying. I know this to be true.

8

We were out on the fields and found a rattlesnake in the
barracks upon our return. It was asleep by the refrigerator.
Wimbledon beat it to death with a broken broom handle
and cut its head off with a pair of garden sheers just to
be sure. He said those things can play dead for days. He
refused to clean the puddle of blood and it dried overnight.
Robert Lee swears he can see the face of Jesus in the dried
blood. Try as I may, I just can't squint enough to agree.

9

The Lady with Long Legs has not been seen all week. We assume she is dead.

Things are changing around here.

10

The General has been hung. His body, like a flag, hangs above head for all to see. His loose bits flap in the wind. His dead eyes watch our every move. The guards are conducting business as usual, as if nothing out of the ordinary has happened. It is not clear why we are all still here. The King is dead. Perhaps we have a new king, or perhaps all the guards and soldiers are doing their duty because nobody has told them to stop. Perhaps they are deep in a groove. Momentum, by nature, is difficult to reverse.

I discussed the state of things with Wimbledon and Robert Lee. We tried to include the brothers, but they ignored us. We have decided that everything will just have to work itself out. We will join the charade and try not to get in the way of any stray bullets. It seems like the safest thing to do. We have also decided to carry machetes at all times. This seems wise. Still, we must retain an air of nonchalance.

11

I was getting high with the mid-morning guard. He says the body is not real. The body that is hanging in the courtyard has been dead for over a year and kept on ice, he says. INTERESTING, I say. THE GENERAL IS NOT DEAD, he says. WE ARE ALL DEAD, I say. EVERYONE HERE IS DEAD.

It's funny, at least to me, how similar heaven and hell really are. How it is really left up to the individual to decide what their surroundings signify to them. How perspective can change at any given moment. How reason does not make sense of life.

The windowsill needs dusting. Perhaps this is hell. The Lady with the Long Legs enters, peacock feather in hand. Perhaps this is heaven. I watch her ass as she moves through the room like an amateur ballerina, like a prepubescent girl dreaming of one day being a ballerina, feather dusting the surfaces. I watch as her thighs brush together at certain strategic crescendos of her dance. I wonder if she is horny. She looks horny.

ARE YOU HORNY RIGHT NOW? I ask. I am sitting in my chair, the one I was sitting in when we met.

The window is closed. She does not reply. She slowly saunters across the room toward me, holding eye contact, methodically snorting all the mucus from deep inside her self, gathering it all in the back of her throat. She carefully spits into my coffee mug.

THAT WAS STILL HOT.

STILL IS.

12

Birds are dying. They began falling out of the sky last week. First one by one, and later in groups. The ones that dropped last week are forming colonies, playing host to insects. The smell is awful. The air is too thick to breathe, like oil.

13

Men are dying. Dropping to their knees and keeling over. So far it's just the guards, but we figure it'll get all of us sooner or later, whatever it is. Most have been found dead. One or two have been seen stumbling and falling. The General's corpse, imposter or not, is swinging in a slight breeze, watching things fall apart. I spent the evening forcing myself to stare at him. Is it him? It looks like him. He is smiling. When the wind blows him toward a certain angle, toward the north, he appears to be laughing.

He appears to be laughing at us.

14

The roses are blooming. The potatoes have broken soil, the leaves are getting fat. The sun takes turns with the rainclouds, giving life so much of what it wants. The light, the water, the light again. This time of year, life inflates almost redundantly. I am bored of it.

Wildlife is blooming at an alarming rate as an invisible plague slowly spreads through humans. The remaining birds are alive and well, the corpses have been swept away and whatever got to them has moved on to us. The doctor lost his wife yesterday. He is our only doctor and he is paralyzed with grief. He is doing no more than going through the motions in our time of need.

The plague has equalized everyone. The guards are no longer the guards. We are all prisoners. We are on the same level. The General still looks down on us from above, losing weight, slowly turning skeletal. Dead-man-smell everywhere. I can't help but realize that it all started with him. I try to remember why they killed him, but I'm drawing a blank. Perhaps I'll ask Wimbledon.

15

I'm getting to the bottom of this. Or the bottom of this is getting to me. Either way.

16

I masturbated seven times in one sitting. It was an experiment. The seventh time took me almost two hours. It was painful, my skin raw, and the orgasm was more like a fart than an orgasm. My cum, a light mist. I didn't even bother cleaning up after myself, I just turned the cushion over. In the end, I wasn't thinking about sex. I wasn't thinking about men and women, which is what I usually think about. I wasn't thinking about people at all, not even myself. I was thinking about a building. A large concrete building with lots of windows, all identical. Right angles, straight lines. I was thinking about symmetry. I was thinking about an idea forming inside a man with a blank piece of paper and a pencil. What it took to get that idea out of the man and onto the paper. What it took to take that paper and turn it back into an idea. What it took to take that idea and build it. To be the first man. To watch the idea mutate into a structure that would provide a thousand homes inside of which people could live and cook and eat and sleep and masturbate. Perhaps one brave soul would masturbate seven times in one sitting. Imagine what he would think about.

17

Robert Lee has eyes like a Norwegian. He is usually a good man for the job, whatever the job may be. Usually. But he is getting weaker and weaker. His eyes are dead.

Dead Norwegian.

18

I am alive, but everybody else is dead.

WHAT HAPPENED TO THE SON OF THE SUN?

We are at war. My family is dead. My best friends are dead. Now it's just me and a clusterfuck of people I don't like. I miss Eric. He was a funny man. I do not miss Pamela's voice, only her body and the way it used to bend. Nobody here is funny anymore. When I look at a body, I see a corpse. When I look at a piece of fruit, I see a corpse. There are no mirrors and no windows.

A baby was born with twelve functional fingers and thirteen functional toes. Many people see her as a sign. A message from god. She is a child of the sun. She has been sent to help. To end the war. To bring back the rain. To bring back fuel. They say she's neo-human. Of the utmost importance. Superior. She is worth more than us or anybody else.

They say she is of the future. She will communicate with more efficiency, she will tell more people what to do. She will kick up dust. Computers will be custom built for her. These computers will be called super computers.

That's what they say.

I say different things. I am of a different faith. I believe that the girl with twelve fingers and thirteen toes is half of a pair. She is half a twin. She shared space inside her mother with another baby, a brother, but the girl was greedy. She wanted more nutrition and she took more of her mother's energy for herself. When the boy was weak enough, she assumed him. Consumed. She swallowed his self into hers.

When she was born, each peasant thanked the sun god one time for each of his daughter's fingers and toes, twenty five thanks in total. Her fingernail clippings like diamonds. Fools fed her everything we had. We offered music to her, our most sacred gift, and she accepted without question. Greedy on the outside as she was inside her mother. By the time we realized we were feeding a monster we were already inside her stomach, shaking hands with her dead brother and his eight fingers and his seven toes.

part five

hologram

Dear Light

Dear Light of Day,

I remember everything. Everything. I remember too much. More than my life. I remember my mother's pregnant belly, ripe like watermelon, fat with laughter. My birth came later than expected. Waiting is the worst. After two weeks of waiting, my father poured her a glass of champagne and they toasted to this life, that life, to the windowsills and waitresses, and they drank. And another. I remember. I was there. I can feel the tingle of the alcohol tiptoeing through her veins. The baby kicked! THE BABY KICKED! We danced together, faster and faster as father packed the bags. Grabbed the keys.

I remember the day Johnny was shot. How Jackie cried and cried.

I remember the Black Forest. The waltzing Matildas, how the fat hung over their ankles. How they wobbled in celebration of themselves. I remember the dirt paths. They went on and on, changing only ever so slightly, as the forest thickened until there was nothing but bark, leaf and darkness. Light of Day, you would not have fit in. They would have strangled you.

I remember the amalgamation. There is a light connecting us all. I am touching my coffee cup, which is touching the table, which is touching the linoleum tiles of the kitchen floor, which is touching the front door, which is touching the cement steps outside the door. The cement steps are touching the pathway, which is touching the street, which, somewhere quite far from here, is touching the beach, which is touching the ocean. You are swimming. The curve of your breaststroke.

I remember school as an institution. The days run away. The words we wrote on the bathroom walls. They didn't like that much, did they? The first drink. A mixture of everything left over by other people. Bright green. I remember the sharing of bodies. Stuff strutting. The flatulence.

My mother's parents' home. The narrow driveway, a bed of gravel between two brick buildings, the black gate, the courtyard. I remember rose gardens. A white dog with black spots that was mean to everyone but my little sister. My little sister! How she whined. How she wore a denim baseball cap and a denim jacket and denim jeans and denim Chuck Taylors, because that's exactly what I wore. How stupid and great we looked! How we loved those clothes. The grass stains on our knees.

I remember the bath time I took a bite of a bar of soap. I cried and cried.

I remember the white cliffs of Dover. The world was made of chalk. Drive the car onto the ferry boat and it takes you over the channel. I remember the first time we went under the water. How disappointed I was that the tunnel was not clear and see-through. I dreamt of shark infested waters. I thought we were going to see bananafish. I wanted that perfect day. I expected them to play cellos and trombones.

I forget the facial structure of my immediate family. White skin blurs slowly coming into focus. But I remember the design of the playground at the bottom of the hill. The slide. The swings. The grey electricity box. The power lines. The wooden climbing frame. Dirty sand.

I remember a boy. His name is Greg. I remember him silly. Limbs flailing, almost animated. Hair just this side of long, flopping over his forehead, into his eyes. He skateboards ugly. He takes a holiday to some place and crashes a boat and dies. I remember washing my hands in California as it happened. Playing tennis alone against a brick wall. The sun soaked bay smiling up from below.

I remember riding the bus to school. I remember each and every bus ride separately. How the drivers hated us. How they waved us on in spite of themselves and their hatred or annoyance. We drew on their steamed windows with our dirty hands and shouted in a language they did not understand.

I remember the autobahn. How slow we felt elsewhere. I remember the autoroute. How they tried to drive us off the road because we had a German car. I remember the homes we rented for the holidays. The photos we only took of smiles. Never a camera out at home, never captured the dull moments or the moments of terror or misery. I don't know what I look like crying, but I know what I look like pretending to smile.

I remember how my maternal grandmother was the first to die. Cancer. How she withered away. The last time I saw her, she was more bone than anything else, but still smiled just as warmly. I tried to say I LOVE YOU, but the words wouldn't come out. I remember my grandfather on the telephone, angry because the nurse was late, shouting into the receiver WELL I THOUGHT THE FACT THAT SHE'S DYING MIGHT GIVE HER SOME PRIORITY and that's when I knew she was actually dying and not just sick, and that's also when I knew that the fact that someone is dying rarely gives them any priority.

I remember my grandfather's medals. How they shined proudly on the walls wrapped around the staircase. Plaques and old photographs. Honors for duties he performed blindly. There is a playground in his village. It is there because he put it there after visiting us and seeing our playground at the bottom of the hill. That's something true and good and it makes people happy.

I remember a man in the village with too much to say. He walks toward the school with an unsteady swagger. The children are in the playground. He says he's there to pick up his kid. The teacher says WHICH KID BELONGS TO YOU. The man says I DON'T CARE, I'll TAKE ANY OF THEM and then he runs. What a creeper. Yeah, definitely a weird guy. He dropped his bottle opener. I picked it up.

I remember graduation ceremonies. Plastic seats, wooden tables, paper trophies, Styrofoam plates. We ate with our hands. How drunk we were on ourselves and our achievement! How happy we were to finally be leaving. Leaving the concrete walls, the tables attached to the chairs and the damn teachers. Damn those teachers to hell! Though most knew not the damage they were doing to our soft minds. Most were victims too. But damn them nonetheless!

I remember that when a child shouts in jubilation it often sounds like a woman in distress. The smell of dogs. How disgusting. Their breath, their farts. Wet fur. Awful creatures.

I remember girlfriends. I know I didn't like the girls as much as I liked the idea of having them. My first lasted three days or so, until I disliked both her and the idea of having her and we parted ways. I have had girlfriends I didn't even talk to. We communicated through concerned third parties and complicated hand gestures. By the time of my first kiss I had a romantic soul, old as oak. I was in America—California of all states. I danced around a warehouse on the other side of El Camino Real with a girl until our tongues touched. The sensation was bizarre. I held it close to my chest and filed it somewhere deep down. It was easy to forget, but also easy to remember.

I expected palm trees. I expected breast enlargements. I expected bleached blonde everything. I expected surf. Tie dye. I did not expect it to be ironic. I saw eucalyptus. Old people in big cars. Brilliant bright teeth, an American smile stretches the cheeks. Americans have perfected the smile to the point of exhaustion, like sometimes I don't ever want to see another one. I watched nice days float in one ear and out the other, watched them through open windows.

I remember sawdust on the floor. Free refills, free peanuts.

I remember the coastline. The bonfires on the beaches of Half Moon Bay and Pacifica. I remember driving on mushrooms, giggling through the mist at midnight or worse. The fog rolls thick down the mountains, filling the valley. I remember the smoke. Filling a parked car until we couldn't see ourselves. Ashing on the floor and all over the back seat. Checkpoint Charlie. Gunther. How to roll a joint. The luxury of a blunt. The love of Northern Californian weed buried deep in our chests, behind our lungs. O, the cheeseburgers we ate!

I remember seeing soldiers for the first time. They looked just like on television. I liked their uniforms and their weapons, but the novelty did not last long. I remember the first time a soldier stole my food. The war that nobody acknowledged was a strange one. We didn't really know if we were invading or being invaded, if we were civilians or soldiers or rebels. Nobody told us what to do, until suddenly they did. This sensation was like being thrown into icy water. After a while, the temperature becomes what's normal. The skin tightens and thickens. Fingernails fall off and grow back. Forty years go by and you are a child with children. These children have grown up to be soldiers in their own wars. Practice makes perfect. Eventually we are fighting a perfect, never-ending war. Casualties keep the doctors and nurses busy. The need for weapons keeps the factories in a constant state of production. The rationing of resources, especially food, keeping us all modest. The thirst that keeps us humble. The patience we develop, the endurance we grow in our collective spinal column. These are the types of scars our children inherit. These scars are passed on from generation to generation. This is called evolution. I remember evolution.

I remember the accident that made me forget. My lover had brown hair. I remember driving. Bright headlights on a rainy night. I remember listening to the Beach Boys, just because it made the kid stop crying. I wish they all could be California girls. I remember remembering my first California girl. How I would love to trade her for my wife. My wife, talking about undercooked vegetables. My wife, mid-gossip. I was thinking about a young girl's vagina. California girls taste like the Pacific Ocean, like broken waves. How easily she came. How she hummed with me in her mouth and held eye contact. How she asked for more. I was always so fully erect. She worked me good. O, how I wish they all could be California girls. They could be. And, suddenly, they are. They are California girls, all of them. And the headlights are flashing by. My California girl is moaning in my ear. The light is orange. Deeper, deeper. The light is orange. I'm going to cum. I am going to cum inside her. The light is red. I do not break. My wife does not see the other car, but for a split second before impact, I do. And I know what's going to happen. And the Beach Boys know what's going to happen. Every girl in California knows what's going to happen. The kid probably knows what's going to happen. My wife remains blissfully unaware. The artichokes were a bit soft, but artichokes can be tricky and wasn't so-and-so's hair ghastly. Yes, darling, it was. And then, it happens.

I remember this. Metal on concrete. Lights. Bright lights and I feel fine. I see a woman lying on the road, her face cut. She is bleeding, not moving. She seems familiar, but I cannot place her. She has brown hair. I remember the kid. I wish I didn't. I feel sorry for whoever I can feel sorry for, not realizing it's me the whole time. I am the one I feel sorry for. Who exactly that is, I do not know.

I know I am sorry. I am sorry for almost everything.
I would like to apologize to the palm trees, those that
burned. I would like to apologize to both my sisters, to
my mother and my father. To my lovers, my friends, The
General. To strangers, animals, clouds and metal and
concrete. I should not be here. I should not have been
there. This should not have been your burden. I should not
have been yours to carry. The fact that I am here frightens
me.

I am so sorry for everything.

I turn away from the window and the world outside.

The oak trees have been swing dancing birds into the wind
but stopped not half a minute ago.

CAJETAN

THE PATRON SAINT OF UNEMPLOYED PEOPLE
DIED OF GRIEF IN THE KINGDOM OF NAPLES
ON THE SEVENTH OF AUGUST
FIFTEEN FORTY SEVEN

THE TWO-HEADED NIGHTINGALE
JO JO THE DOG FACED BOY
CHANG THE CHINESE GIANT
PRINCE RADIAN THE LIMBLESS MAN

THESE PEOPLE NEVER PRAYED TO SAINT CAJETAN
BUT STAGGERED THROUGH THE BARRIO
TO BEG HIS BROTHER
FOR A CIGARETTE BREAK

PLEASE
TAKE ME OUT TO DINNER
LIFT MY LIVER TO THE HEAVENS AND SQUEEZE
I WANT TO WATCH YOUNG PEOPLE FALL IN LOVE

MY LUNGS, A CRIPPLED BIRD
MY HEART BEATS YOUR FIST
I AM PAPER, YOU ARE FIRE
DON'T MAKE ME GO OUT THERE AGAIN TONIGHT

JO JO THE DOG FACED BOY
FLUENTLY SPOKE FOUR LANGUAGES
BUT ALL ANYONE EVER WANTED TO HEAR
WAS A BARK

FOLLOWED BY A BARK
FOLLOWED BY A BARK
FOLLOWED BY A BARK
FOLLOWED BY A BARK

FOLLOWED BY A BARK
FOLLOWED BY A BARK
FOLLOWED BY A BARK
FOLLOWED BY A BARK

FOLLOWED BY A BARK

amateur pornography

poems

MY CREDENTIALS

1.

I have watched a woman die.
I have listened to the rhythm of her breathing slow
and kept time tapping my fingernail against the edge of the
last bottle of bourbon she ever finished
and finished the last bottle of bourbon she ever opened
and I have waited patiently.

2.

I have had sexual relations with a person and been in love
with that same person at the same time.

3.

I have played the piano drunk.

PRACTICE

To mourn the deaths of your loved ones
whilst they are still alive. This is called practice.

The neighborhood celebrates the death of the coyote
that has been killing house cats.

House cats guilty of being house cats.
The coyote guilty of being a coyote.

Humans guilty, of course.
To celebrate death is forgivable.

The coyote was hit by a man who lives alone.
He masturbates quietly thinking of

his high school English teacher.
This is called practice.

He lies in bed with his eyes open, waiting for sleep,
thinking about the coyote.

He grows jealous of the dead animal.
He would trade places in a heartbeat.

He misses his dead friends.
He misses his married friends.

He misses his English teacher and the way her tits would
jiggle every time she subjugated.

He mourns his mother, who is alive and well and married
to a man named Bruce.

As he begins to weep, the ghost of the coyote
appears out of nowhere and whispers

YOU MOTHERFUCKER! I WOULD NOT TRADE
PLACES WITH YOU

IN A MILLION YEARS and the man cries and cries into
his pillow.

He does not remember his dreams.
He wakes with an erection.

He drinks his coffee black
and drives to work listening to Billy Joel

having learned nothing.
Nothing at all.

GOSPEL

The metal in teeth sings
Mississippi delta

with egg yolk dried on the crotch.
The apostles gather at the foot of her bed.

This is where the pervert feels at home.
The empty space up skirt.

Most men idealize the breasts they have touched.
Some mediocre, remembered as rainclouds
or the cheeks of opera singers.

The metal in teeth holds
its breath. A hand touches a knee.
A stranger starts asking a question
at the bus stop.

CYPRUS

There is heaven and hell
but there is also Birmingham.

There is North Frodingham
where my grandfather is dying slowly.

Heaven is behind the curtains
but so are windows and dead flies.

Hell is other people
but so are orgasms and contagious yawns.

Other people hang laundry like the enemy
and watch television holding milkshakes

and go to jail for being mistaken
and eat and drink all kinds of shit.

My grandmother shot herself in the foot in Cyprus.
It was an accident that still makes us laugh.

THE BUTCHER'S HOOK

In Singapore business is booming.
Men wearing cream-colored suits

drink fluorescent cocktails singing
There's Only One Team in London as

other men are wearing Chelsea blue at
The Butcher's Hook, eating

a pint of prawns, steak frites, drinking
a snifter of Ardbeg. It's a celebration.

A piss up over a table of old oak.
A baby asleep upstairs.

Taxi back to Adelaide. A nice Afghani driver
takes the scenic route, chats, points out

the riot police, the rude boys, the lads.
It's difficult to tell the hooligans

from the hooligans, I think we laugh.
"It's always the same," he says. "Home games.

That's why I swear by Match
of the Day. Life's safer on television."

There are chicken bones all over the pavement.
Everywhere we look, there's a pub closing early.

THE PRIDE OF WHATEVER

I remember my Grandmother's hair a nest
the same shade as the White Cliffs.

Before the tunnel was built
we would catch the ferry from

Calais to Dover or the other way round. The P&O,
Peninsular and Oriental, the Pride of whatever.

I stood on deck with Dad
and he pointed toward the cliffs,

told me about the chalk, the flint
and quartz, the ghosts of planktonic algae.

His beard the way it was
I always assumed him Captain

and me first mate. Or fossils.
Both of us, fossils.

UPON MEETING A COYOTE

There is a triangle in your neighborhood
where a coyote lives
on house cats.

I ride my bicycle to work
past all the photocopied posters,
fading.

One morning I came face to face with her
we almost touched wet noses
right along the hypotenuse

surrounded by fog or mist.
She didn't seem real.
I mistook her for a dog

and tried to run my hand
along the flat of her forehead
but her fur was too short.

A SATURDAY AFTERNOON

When weather permits
dogs lie on the lawn
to watch gardeners

plant plants and tend to them.
Dogs lick genitals and breathe deeply.
You cannot ask for more

from a Saturday afternoon
as cheap beer drives itself home
and the birds still singing,

their beaks yawning apart
as if they might laugh
if they could understand.

THE MASON JAR

Thanks to sweaty palms
the mason jar slips.

The mason jar in pieces
and you

so quick to play it cool
work quickly

with bare hands
backwards.

This is a poem where the title comes at the end
and theres no punctuation The mistakes are apparently

deliberate
I stole this

idea from some Clyde I never met I
bought the world's largest vacuum

Its so big I had to buy a miniature
version of it to vacuum its insides A

grown man can curl up comfortably
inside the dust bag which is exactly

where my lover found me
as she attempted to vacuum

a spilt milkshake Afterwards
we had sex The title is

A GREAT DAY

PLATEAU

We reached a plateau

where everyone's parents died
except yours and mine.

Mine,
too polite.

Your mother
too afraid of your father
and your father
too much of an asshole.

Clinging to life by fingernail and bucktooth
using a combination of rage and racism,
blaming it on California and the sun,
taking it out on the family.

The most valuable lesson
he ever taught you and your brothers
was that even in Orange county
there is always something to do.

FAMILY

My mother used to carve
Day of the Dead skulls
out of avocado pits
using a butter knife.

A single sculpture could take anything
from an afternoon
to a fortnight, depending
on the details.

She often
sent them away
to celebrities and
politicians.

She got a thank you note
from George Harrison once,
which she had laminated and kept
in a wooden box with her baby teeth.

I found the box
dust-covered and cold
and threw it in the bonfire last Guy Fawkes
without thinking.

I wish I hadn't done that.

BOMB CLEANERS

After the bomb makers
have finished the making,
they enjoy fresh strawberries

and the cleaners
roll up their sleeves
and polish the bomb shiny.

This is an important part of the process.
Nobody wants to drop a dirty bomb, thus
the cleaning.

A bomb cleaner gets paid
considerably more than a school teacher.

When the bomb is so clean
that the boss could eat his lunch off it,
the bomb cleaners enjoy

whatever is left of
the strawberries

and everybody goes home
to bask in the peaceful terrorism
of house cats.

WINK

When my mother winked at me
last week, it was so slight, the tiniest
twitch of cheek such that her eye
did not quite close—a mosquito lick,
an abandoned shoe—and her,
being my mother, being so English,
drinking ginger wine after a roast
and telling a conversational lie,
a good lie, smiling comfortably.

THE PATRON SAINT'S FEATHER DUSTER

is a necessity
because,
though her life
has been touched
by the fingertips
of god, I guess, dust
still settles
on her
mantelpiece.

Dust
she cannot
pray away.

GHOST BIKE AND SOMETHING ELSE ABOUT DEATH

A famous Viennese prostitute died of meningitis and a
Russian tightrope walker died of self-inflicted castration

and

there is a pure white bicycle by the side of the road.
That means somebody died there too. Some bicycle rider.

A haunting monument to the fragility of life
or a bicycle gone to waste. Somebody

could ride that to work or to
their cousin's house. We should all

visit each other more often or at least
talk on the telephone or something. We ride

bikes, I guess. Anything could happen. A crippled bird
could land on your shoulder.

DUMB DUMB

If you don't love me anymore, that's alright.

Some snake in shallow water
is not waiting for your ankle,
it's just being a snake.

As if all the years could be balanced
by the instinctual dumbness of animals
or blame could be placed upon teeth.

I have worn no clothes but I have never been naked
and nailed to a traffic light or a bus stop.

The newspaper very rarely reads me.

I smear all this shit everywhere
because these days either dance, honestly and literally,
or they start at the very bottom of an ocean of leprosy and
sink lower,
further away from bicycles and Indian food and church
substitute and clouds.

Whatever sleeps between your two slices of white bread,
may it crunch and salt just right for you

and the empty space left in your stomach
will be a monument to the failed meat of those
dumb dumb animals.

ALL DAY

A rain dance of dead
bodies. A bathtub overflowing.
A piano that plays itself
in a mall. All day
at work I think about
your thighs humming like a
refrigerator, buzzing like blonde hair.

Row me a boat. A
small island with a lighthouse.
I envy lonely men with
all their sadness and autumn
to shake at a windowsill,
to ignore the curtains.

I think I am going to die
drinking a glass of milk.

WITH AN EMPTY SEAT NEXT TO ME

I want to die
a strawberry

eaten by some mouth.
Some child's mouth

with baby teeth
and a tiny tongue.

My blood mistaken
for the juice of the fruit

running down the chin
dripping onto a clean white shirt.

Today, three days
after the full moon,

I said the same kind word
to a bus driver and

a librarian. A
swell of human

niceness. I checked out
a book from the one

and the other
drove me home

as I read.
The bus passed

a graveyard.
I thought

about a dead
man crowing at

sunrise and I
thought about

blue lace.
I thought about knees and

how perfect they are.

WORK IS EVERYDAY

You kiss
the dead man's forehead.

The dead man is
your father. The

next day you feel like
you can't go to work

but you go anyway and it's
just like normal, like

work is
everyday.

For lunch, a
cold sandwich.

TERRY

Just thinking of those dead dogs floating down the river, in amongst the wilting palm trees and it's scary how fast snakes can swim. There are cars in the water, fully submerged. I don't suppose they're worth much anymore, what with all the rust. The bloated backseats and the airbags and the seat belts and whatever was stashed in the glove compartment. Virgin Mary dancing on the dashboard, holding her breath. Sweet Jane cassette. All the things we once tried to love have made themselves invisible or, at the very least, hidden. They have become things we are merely trying to tolerate. It will rain and rain forever. We will let the rain fill our eye sockets.

TROY

A lot has happened since you died.

I am north now.
I floated upstream.
I drank a thousand bottles.
I developed a taste for cheap.
I ignored a talkative stranger on the bus.
I kissed my drunk girl.
I danced my tarantella.
I rode my bicycle through the rain.
I complicated a relatively simple thing.
I bamboozled a chieftain.
I shortchanged the laughingstock.
I crossfaded some leopardskin.
I emptied the pillbox.
I churched into an empty room.
I lifted my palms toward the dark cloud.
I sharpened my prayer tooth.
I whittled my hambone.
I snagged the downpour.
I set fire to one end.
I sucked the other.
I fucked my clenched fist.
I took it easy on the weatherman.
I found a silver fishing knife on a pier in Santa Barbara.
I deflected Sweden and remembered Geneva

but

I never went to Boston and
I never broke.

NATHANIEL

I held grief
in a paper cup,
covered with
my weak palm
and I mourned
into the abyss.

In the
presence
of your open
casket
I wanted to kiss
your dead face

until everything was wet.

KATHERINE

Last year
nobody would have guessed
how quickly we would all forget
and move on.

Since you died,
five other people
have died here and
many more elsewhere,
obviously.

You,
bulldog of cat loving woman,
would chuckle rather
than dance,
always barking
the same song.

WILLIAM

You drank
a bottle of whiskey a day
for days and days.

When Muhammad
came to town
he called you up
and some lucky lady

snorted a line of coke
off his bedside table
before you and he
shared her

the way other people,
normal, nice people,
share sandwiches
or cigarettes.

The ways she could
bend would have made
a stockbroker
blush.

Years later
you cared so much
but didn't give
anything.

JULIA

A woman
sifts through
a strange man's
oak chest
searching for
a photograph.

Later
she is outside and
it is dark

and when she
burns
the
photograph

she feels
much better.

Her fingers
warm.

JOEL

There are
a thousand
rose petals

covering
the windshield
of your father's

Cadillac
and the dogs
are going

wild. I do
not trust
you.

You are
bad meat.
Your

low profile
casts a
coffin shaped

shadow
over the
wallpaper

in the kid's
room, but still
there is

something
about you
worth

keeping.
Whatever. Let's
smoke inside.

AMANDA

I am listening
to soft music
at night in my
bedroom.

I know some-
time you will
grab me and

take me home
with you.

Maybe I will
be your
next girlfriend

and Diane will
be around to
help. This will
take time, but

I am listening to
soft music,
being patient, waiting
for you.

What is
this about
sleeping through
the end of the world?

What is
wrong with
you, Barry?

I hate to do this
because I love you, but
I hate you, Barry, and

agony is
the same old
song.

I am com-
ing to New
York City
on Sunday

and leaving
on Thursday.

Please
grab me. Please
come to my
hotel room and I will

ask Diane to
be my new
mother. My mother
died in 1984.

You are in
the dog house.

I hope you
will always
live in California.

I like most
of your music
except Copacaba-
na and Some

Kind of
Friend, but
I love you and

I know
I will
see you
someday.

We were
more Irish
than Russian
in May

and Jewish in
August and

developed
Ester's nose
in April.

It formed in
one week.

If you and I get married,
Diane could
stay around

to help. We
will have
a happy
home.

I am getting
close to
something. It

could happen
any day
now.

Please call
me on my
telephone. We
need to talk.

Life is
too short,
somebody
said.

Don't wait
until it is
too late. I am

going back
to Florida.
I am going

back to New
York in
April. On

Sunday
I will
be gone

with coffee
and pop.
There is

a nice
heat and we
are engaged
to be

married.
I have a
surprise
for you,

Barry. On April
Fools' Day,
it's my
birthday.

I am old. I am
worried about
you, Barry.
Drive to me.

CRAIG

We'd get
so wet
it hurt.

Back when
the most holy thing
was wheels,

to get
wet
was some

kind of cancer.
A houseplant
trusting

a clock,
like some kids
can't tell

when they're hungry,
the tummy
just never

rumbles,
I guess, so
they just cry

and cry
without knowing
what for.

JOHN

Gang
of slug
upturned

trying to push
the rain
back

into the sky
and the pigeons
singing.

All night
I was
pretending

to sleep,
thinking—what
would

I do
without
you?

MATT

Hating on
the dust
like, damn,

can't you
just
fucking

sweep
yourself?
This hair

keeps
growing
out of

my face,
my head,
the pits

under
my arms
and

all around
my
crotch. It's

weird. The
crotch hair is
thicker,

more coarse
than what's
on my

head. Our
mistakes
feed

on the
moss of
Monday

mornings,
but I'd wager
the rest of

my lemonade
that things
work out

just fine.

FLORA

On the bus
I sat next to
a drag queen.

She was wearing
your
perfume.

I thought of
your collarbone
and your shoulder blade

and I remembered
crashing
your mother's

car
into a wall
in Strasbourg.

MARK

Ever since
we found
that dead body

washed up
on the
riverbank,

every
river
I see

feels empty.
Just water,
water,

boring water.

RICHARD

Some
miracle drugs
slap dance

through
the ventricles
like a naive

Charles
with new
shoes.

LEE

You are depressed in heaven.

You want to die,
so you die

over and over and over.

And over.

And over.

about the author

Robert Duncan Gray is always celebrating something.

One time, circa 1993, Rob was a real asshole to someone who was riding a bicycle.

Since starting his work with HOUSEFIRE, Rob has become dependant upon the following narcotic substances:

Cashmere
Yage
Courvoisier
Secret Sauce
Dim Sum
Mexican Cola and so on, you get it.

Rob would like to take this opportunity to thank you:

Thank you.

HOUSE FIRE

housefirebooks.com

www.ingramcontent.com/pod-product-compliance
Lightning Source LLC
Chambersburg PA
CBHW061237170626
46809CB00007B/2722

* 9 7 8 1 9 3 7 3 9 5 0 3 2 *